3 8538 00002 7610

P9-DNE-207

E
LEWIS, J. Patrick
Night of the goat children

(A)

36269

STOCKTON
Township Public Library
Stockton, IL

Books may be drawn for two weeks and renewed once
A fine of five cents a library day shall be paid for each
book kept overtime.

Borrower's card must be presented whenever a book is
taken If card is lost a new one will be given for payment of
50 cents.

Each borrower must pay for damage to books.

KEEP YOUR CARD IN THIS POCKET

DEMCO

Night of the Goat Children

J. Patrick Lewis

Pictures by Alexi Natchev

Dial Books for Young Readers  New York

Published by Dial Books for Young Readers
A member of Penguin Putnam Inc.
375 Hudson Street • New York, New York 10014

Text copyright © 1999 by J. Patrick Lewis
Pictures copyright © 1999 by Alexi Natchev
All rights reserved • Designed by Nancy R. Leo
Printed in Hong Kong on acid-free paper
First Edition
1 3 5 7 9 10 8 6 4 2

Library of Congress Cataloging in Publication Data
Lewis, J. Patrick.
Night of the goat children / by J. Patrick Lewis; pictures by Alexi Natchev.—1st ed.
p.   cm.
Summary: Birgitta, the brave princess, asks five children to disguise themselves as immortal
goats and outsmart a dangerous band of outlaws threatening to take over the land.
ISBN 0-8037-1870-5 (trade). —ISBN 0-8037-1871-3 (lib. bdg.)
[1. Princesses—Fiction. 2. Disguise—Fiction. 3. Goats—Fiction.]
I. Natchev, Alexi, ill. II. Title.
PZ7.L5866Ni 1999   [E]—dc20   95-45186   CIP   AC

The art was rendered with acrylics, with some accents of collage,
on a handmade cotton paper.

To Peter and Helen Neumeyer
J. P. L.

For Nancy Leo, with many thanks
A. N.

10-6-99   36269

ONCE LONG AGO, a wicked band of outlaws blew like the cold north wind across the land. They looted every town that stood in their path, and now laid siege to a little kingdom called Beda, deep in the Black Forest.

The king of Beda was too old to rule and had wisely given his throne to his only daughter, Birgitta. Both clever and bold, she was soon known as Birgitta the Brave. As brave as she might be, however, she was no match for a hundred outlaws and their leader, Ubo Skald, who wore a horned helmet and a gold ring through his nose— a man-bull if there ever was one.

Beda was protected from invaders by a wall thirty feet high and four feet thick that surrounded the town. Now when the goatherds and shepherds heard the thunder of horses' hooves, they drove their flocks through the entrance, and locked the iron gates behind them.

"Fools of Beda!" shouted Ubo Skald. "Give us your animals—or we will destroy you!"

No answer came from inside the kingdom but the bleating of sheep and goats.

The outlaws heaved ropes and grappling hooks up the wall face, but before they could climb to the top, Beda guards sliced their ropes in two. Down, down the thieves fell, into the weeds and the tall grass—or headlong into the creek running nearby.

"Peasants!" cried Ubo Skald. "You will see there is no way out!" With that, the outlaws retreated. They made camp within arrows' shot of the wall, and went to sleep.

The next morning Ubo Skald ordered his men to cut down three tall trees to use as battering rams. "If you can't go over the wall, then go through it!" he commanded. Again and again his men—ten to each tree—charged the stone fortress, but the iron gates refused to budge. When the weary invaders finally fell back, all was silent except for the constant cries of sheep and goats.

There was no way for the outlaws to get inside the walls, and the townspeople dared not escape. Nor could they take their flocks outside to graze. So the thieves returned to their camp, and waited for Beda to surrender.

That night Princess Birgitta, afraid for her people, called the elders to her side. "Sheep and goats are both our pride and our food. If the animals starve from lack of water and grazing, then we will starve with them. What is to be done?"

The old men scratched their snow-white beards and wagged their heads like clock pendulums.

"Pray," counseled the first.

"Run," said the second.

"Surrender?" whispered the third.

Birgitta weighed carefully the advice of the elders, then decided on a plan of her own.

"Skin six fat goats," she said. "Shear twenty woolly sheep, and bring me five children full of pluck and mischief."

"Brilliant plan, my lady!" "Bold strategy!" "Stroke of genius!" exclaimed the three elders, though they hadn't the slightest idea what Birgitta was up to.

An hour later the children—Elise, Kattrin, Hans, Bertold, and little Marta—stood before the princess in their nightclothes, half-asleep and grumbling.

"I will reward each of you if you stay awake with me tonight," said Birgitta, "to do battle with Ubo Skald."

"Us against the outlaw?" exclaimed Elise.

"The man-bull?!" gasped Kattrin.

"He'll squash us like bugs!" cried Bertold.

"May I be excused?" said Hans.

"But what can *we* do against Ubo Skald?" little Marta asked.

The princess drew them closer. "Listen very carefully, my children. . . ."

Later that night, on Birgitta's instructions, the guards lit lanterns along the high wall, then quickly disappeared inside Beda. A full moon, owl eyes, and the outlaws' wood fires shone around the forest. Into the gloom of black shadows the princess, disguised as a filthy hag dressed in tatters, slipped out of the kingdom and made her way across the clearing toward the enemy camp. No sooner had she lighted her lamp—and noisily cracked a branch—than she was captured and taken before Ubo Skald.

"What have you got in that rotten sack, woman?" he growled.

"Mushrooms. Been diggin' them since dusk!" she lied, stepping forward boldly. "And what's your business here, thief-with-a-gold-nose?"

"Before the sun sets thrice, this besieged kingdom will be mine!"

Birgitta cackled, "You must be mad or cursed—or both!"

"Stop jabbering, hag. What do I have to fear from these simpleton shepherds, eh? They'll be begging for bread and water soon enough!"

"Three secrets I know well," Birgitta said. "One, behind those walls lives a princess with a heart of stone. A sorceress without equal."

"Sorcery?" the outlaws murmured, for one thief was more superstitious than the next.

"Two," said Birgitta, "by some strange magical power, their animals refuse to die!"

"Magical power!" the men muttered, the words running like mad mice through the jittery camp.

But Ubo Skald only laughed. "A cunning princess. Immortal animals! And what might be your third terrifying secret, Lady Ugly?"

"Ah, come closer, thieves. Some tales must not be told," Birgitta hissed, "or the teller, it is said, will pay with her life! So keep this to yourselves: The woods whisper that the witch princess of Beda can turn humans into goats!"

Ubo Skald's men shrank back, afraid of nothing on land or sea . . . except a witch's curse!

"Tie her to a birch pole!" Ubo Skald ordered. "We'll roast her on a spit, and the devil himself will thank us for it!"

"Aiiiyyeee!" Birgitta shrieked. Her signal to the town pierced the night. And there across the clearing, the outlaws could see five goats parading atop the fortress lit by the high lanterns.

"Shoot them!" Ubo commanded. Instantly dozens of arrows struck the whiskered goats.

But no billy goat fell. Stuffed under their pelts were five layers of the finest wool, and under the thick wool, protected from the arrows, were Elise, Kattrin, Hans, Bertold, and little Marta. On hands and knees, they crawled along the parapet unharmed, stuck with so many arrows they looked like pincushions.

"*Bah,*" Elise sang in a billy goat voice.

"*Bah-ha,*" cried Marta and Kattrin even louder.

"*Bah-ha-ha,*" Hans and Bertold bleated louder still, mocking the thieves.

"The hag s-speaks the truth!" one bandit stammered. "The princess of Beda *is* a sorceress! And their animals *do* refuse to d-die!" Even Ubo Skald shuddered to see the stuck goats still prancing and butting heads on the high wall.

But that was not the end of Birgitta's cleverness. Amidst the confusion she slipped away into the dark woods she knew so well. Inside her sack there were no mushrooms at all. Only an animal skin! A few paces from the enemy camp she knelt down, took the goat overcoat out of the sack, and wrapped it around her.

Now, thought Birgitta, my third secret will be revealed! Crawling to the light of a single moonbeam shining through the trees, she bleated. "Help me, you fools! I'm only a poor mushroom maid! Save me from the wicked princess of *Beh-he-he-eda!* Save me, Skald. *Beh-eh-eh-eh!*"

"The hag told the truth!" cried Ubo Skald, staring in horror at the moonlit spot. "The witch princess of Beda *did* change the old woman into a she-goat!" He brandished his sword against the unseen dread. "And we may be next!"

"Save yourself, goat woma-a-a . . ." he began, but at that moment terror rippled the flanks of his white charger, who snorted once and bolted from the very spot where he stood. Ubo Skald desperately seized the stallion's mane. And like some gigantic bird, horse and rider went flapping into the night.

A hundred terrified horsemen followed, flying from Beda at a furious gallop, only to disappear in their own dust as if fear itself had spirited them away.

Princess Birgitta shed her disguises and watched the whirlwind vanish through the forest, then hurried home to the tiny kingdom where Beda's gates swung wide!

First to greet her were the three good-hearted elders. "Brilliant plan, your highness!" "Bold strategy!" "Stroke of genius!" they repeated, although they hadn't the slightest idea what really had happened.

So the princess told the story of Ubo Skald and the three secrets. Then she turned to the five children still making mischief in their goat disguises. "As a reward for your bravery," she said, "the kingdom of Beda will hold a celebration every year in your honor."

And even though the hour was late, a lavish feast was prepared. Dancing and singing went on till dawn. It was to be the very first Night of the Goat Children, and many more would follow in the years to come. To the delight of all who were there, Elise, Kattrin, Hans, Bertold, and little Marta the Brave bleated once more the billy goat songs that saved a kingdom—and frightened away the mighty Ubo Skald, who was never heard from again.

Author's Note

This story was inspired by and is loosely based on an actual event. During the Thirty Years War (1618-1648) the Swedes invaded the German countryside, laying siege to the walled town of Beda. They intended to starve the citizens into surrender and were nearly successful. But the inhabitants managed to outsmart the Swedes by sewing together pelts of goats that they had eaten. Children put on these goat disguises and paraded along the high city walls to convince the invaders that Beda was well-stocked with food. The Swedes fell for the trick and retreated.

Today along the "Walkplatz" (town square) stands the Goat Fountain, commemorating with bronze replicas the brave "goat children" of Beda.